For Eleanor Troth &
Emily Peopall
~ *J.S.*

For Jane,
who *loves* Christmas!
~ *T.W.*

First published in the United States 1998 by Little Tiger Press,
N16 W23390 Stoneridge Drive, Waukesha, WI 53188
Originally published in Great Britain 1998 by Magi Publications, London
Text © 1998 Julie Sykes   Illustrations © 1998 Tim Warnes
All rights reserved.
Library of Congress Cataloging-in-Publication Data
Sykes, Julie.
Hurry, Santa! / by Julie Sykes ; illustrated by Tim Warnes.   p.   cm.
Summary : When his alarm clock fails to go off, Santa oversleeps on
Christmas Eve and then encounters a series of disasters that threaten
to prevent him from delivering his presents on time.
ISBN 1-888444-37-1 (hc)
1. Santa Claus—Juvenile Fiction. [1. Santa Claus—Fiction.
2. Christmas—Fiction.]   I. Warnes, Tim. ill.   II. Title.
PZ7.S98325Hu 1998 [E]—dc21 97-51133 CIP AC
Printed in Belgium   First American edition   1 3 5 7 9 10 8 6 4 2

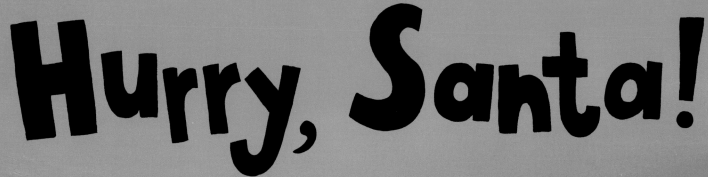

Hurry, Santa!

by Julie Sykes

Pictures by Tim Warnes

It was Christmas Eve, Santa's busiest time of year. But Santa was fast asleep, snoring under his blanket.

"Wake up!" squeaked Santa's little mouse, tugging at his beard. "Hurry, Santa! You can't be late tonight."

"Ouch!" cried Santa, sitting up and rubbing his chin. "Goodness, is that clock right? The alarm didn't go off, and I've overslept."

Santa leapt out of bed and began to pull
on his clothes. He was in such a hurry that
he put both feet in one pant leg and fell flat
on his face.

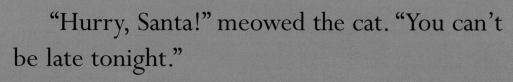

"Hurry, Santa!" meowed the cat. "You can't be late tonight."

"No, I can't," agreed Santa, getting back up. "I can't be late delivering the presents."

When he was finally dressed, Santa hurried
outside to his sleigh. He picked up the harness
and tried to put it on the reindeer.

But the reindeer weren't there!

"Oh no!" cried Santa. "Where can they be?"

"The reindeer are loose in the woods," called Fox.
"You'd better catch them before they wander off.
Hurry, Santa, you can't be late tonight."
"No, I can't," agreed Santa, running toward the trees.

Deep in the woods some
of the reindeer were having a
snowball fight.

"Aaaaah!" shouted Santa as
a snowball hit him in the face.

"Hurry, Santa," hooted Owl. "You don't have time to play in the snow."

"But I wasn't playing!" said Santa.

He searched all over for the other reindeer, but they were nowhere to be found. "I hope you four can pull the sleigh by yourselves," he said. "Come on, we've got work to do."

At last Santa took off, steering
the sleigh toward the moon.
"Go, Reindeer, go!" he shouted.
"We can't be late tonight!"

Around the world they flew, delivering their presents.

"Down again," called Santa, turning the sleigh toward a farm.

"Hurry, Santa!" answered the reindeer. "We're miles from anywhere, and the night's almost over."

"I'm doing my best," boomed Santa, flicking the reins.

Before he knew what was happening,
the reindeer quickened their pace.
"Whoa," Santa cried, but it was too late.
Landing with a bump, the sleigh skidded
crazily across the snow.
"Ooooooh deeeaaar!" cried Santa.

CRASH!
The sleigh had gotten stuck in a giant
snowdrift. Santa scrambled to his feet and rubbed
his bruised bottom. "Nothing broken," he said.
"But we must hurry!"

When the reindeer had untangled themselves,
they tried to dig out the sleigh. They tugged and
pulled and pushed as hard as they could, but the
sleigh was completely stuck in the snow.

"It's no use," wailed the reindeer. "We can't move this sleigh on our own."

"We must keep trying," said Santa. "The sky is getting lighter, and we're running out of time."

Suddenly Santa heard a loud neigh. Trotting toward them was a very large horse.

"Hurry, Santa!" she neighed. "You've still got presents to deliver. *I'll* help you move your sleigh."

So they all pulled together, even Santa's little mouse, but it was no good. The sleigh was still stuck.

"Hurry, Santa!" called the rooster from the barnyard.
"It's nearly morning."

"I am *trying* to hurry," puffed Santa. "One more pull,
everyone!"

At last the sleigh began to move. . . .

And Santa tumbled backward, cheering loudly.

"Hurry, Santa!" called all the animals. "The sun's rising. You've got to finish your rounds before the children wake up."

"Yes," agreed Santa. "It's nearly Christmas Day!"

It was a close call, but by dawn Santa had managed
to deliver every present. Finally, he and the reindeer
arrived back at the North Pole.

"We did it!" yawned Santa. "I wasn't—"

He stopped talking and stared at his sack in dismay. At the very bottom was a present.

"Oh no, how awful!" he cried. "I've forgotten someone!"

Then Santa saw that all the animals were laughing at him.

"That present is for *you*," said the reindeer. "It's from all of us."

"Hurry, Santa!" added the little mouse. "You should open your present. It's Christmas Day!"

"Yes, I should," chuckled Santa. "Now, I wonder what it is. . . . "